The SECRET SPELL BOOK

Adapted by Tom Rogers

Based on the episode "Spellbound," written by Tom Rogers
for the series created by Craig Gerber

Illustrated by the Disney Storybook Art Team

DISNEP PRESS

Los Angeles • New York

First Paperback Edition, February 2017 10 9 8 7 6 5 4 3
ISBN 978-1-4847-4793-3
FAC-029261-18096
Library of Congress Control Number: 2016952301

Printed in the United States of America
For more Disney Press fun, visit www.disneybooks.com

SUSTAINABLE
FORESTRY
INITIATIVE

Certified Sourcing
www.sfiprogram.org
SFI-01415

Today Princess Elena is going to make her friend Mateo the royal wizard of Avalor!

Elena has invited guests from all over
Avalor to attend the ceremony.

As the crowd gets bigger, Mateo gets
nervous. He accidentally drops his
tamborita.
"What if I'm not good enough to be
royal wizard?" Mateo asks.

"You're going to be great," Elena says, handing back his drum-wand. "After all, your grandfather was a royal wizard, too!"

While everyone is watching the
ceremony, an evil wizard named
Fiero sneaks into the castle.
He is there to steal a secret spell book.

Fiero prowls a back hallway,
searching for the spell book.
A guard sees him. "Halt!" he shouts.
But Fiero draws his *tamborita* and
turns the guard into a statue.

The guests in the ballroom
hear the commotion.
Fiero thinks they might try to stop him.
So he turns them all into statues!

When Mateo sees Fiero, he recognizes him. Before Fiero can turn his friends into statues, Mateo casts a spell to protect them.

Mateo knows Fiero is searching for
the spell book.
"We must find the spell book before
he does!" Mateo tells his friends.

Mateo takes out his grandfather's journal. "It says here the spell book is hidden somewhere in the palace." Suddenly, three clues to three keys magically appear on the page.

The first clue leads them to a grandfather clock. When Elena moves the clock hands, a hidden drawer opens. There's a key inside!

The second clue takes them to the music room. As Gabe plays the piano, a secret compartment pops open. "I found the second key!" he exclaims.

The third clue leads them to a painting
of Avalor Bay.
Mateo finds the last key hidden in the
picture frame.

Mateo looks closely at the painting.
"Those weird little caves look
like keyholes," he says.
They insert the keys into the
painting, and it swings open!

Behind the painting, they find a
magical wizard's workshop.
"Look! The secret spell book is
inside," says Mateo.

"I'll take that!" says someone behind them. It's Fiero!

Fiero zaps the spell book with his *tamborita*, and it flies right into his hands!

Gabe and Naomi try to grab the book from Fiero. But the evil wizard turns them into statues.

Then Fiero aims his *tamborita* at
Princess Elena.

"Mateo!" Elena shouts. "You can
beat him!"

Mateo will not let Fiero hurt Princess Elena. *"No!"* he yells angrily. Mateo bangs his *tamborita* and shouts a spell. It blocks Fiero's curse and sends him flying through the door!

Fiero can't believe Mateo had the power to stop him! "But I still have what I came for," he says, running away with the spell book.

"I'm going after Fiero," Mateo says, giving Elena a bottle of magic potion. She uses it to unfreeze Gabe and Naomi.

Mateo chases Fiero through the castle
and into the courtyard.

Fiero aims his *tamborita* and fires a
magic curse at Mateo.

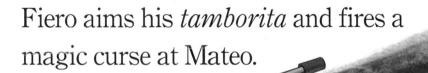

But Mateo blocks the curse with
another spell.

Fiero's own curse bounces back at
him, turning him into a statue!

Just then, Elena, Naomi, and Gabe race
out of the castle to join Mateo. "You
did it, Mateo!" Elena cries happily.
Mateo shrugs. "I guess I did!" he says.

They run back to the ballroom. Mateo blasts the bottle of magic potion with his *tamborita*. The potion showers down on the guests, unfreezing them all!

"I'm proud of you, Mateo," says Elena. "You stopped Fiero and saved the secret spell book."

Mateo blushes. "You believed in me when I didn't even believe in myself," he says. "Thank you."

Then the new royal wizard treats
everyone to a magical fireworks show!